D0536092

NO LONGER
SEATTLE PUBLIC LIBRARY

Southwest Branch

JUL 12 2011

9010 35th Ave SW
Seattle, WA 98126-3821

POST CARD

THIS SPACE MAY BE USED FOR
PRINTED OR WRITTEN MATTER

For
Oleander Grrrabbit
(because I love you)
and the pottery pals
(because I promised)

XXX

SIMON & SCHUSTER BOOKS FOR YOUNG READERS
An imprint of Simon & Schuster Children's Publishing Division
1230 Avenue of the Americas, New York, New York 10020
Copyright © 2005 by Emily Gravett
Originally published in Great Britain in 2005 by Macmillan Children's Books, a division of Mac-
millan Publishers Limited
First U.S. edition 2006

All rights reserved, including the right of reproduction in whole or in part in any form.
SIMON & SCHUSTER BOOKS FOR YOUNG READERS is a trademark of Simon & Schuster, Inc.

The text for this book is set in Bodoni.
The illustrations for this book are rendered in multimedia.
Manufactured in China
4 6 8 10 9 7 5 3
CIP data for this book is available from the Library of Congress.
ISBN-13: 978-1-4169-1491-4
ISBN-10: 1-4169-1491-9

Rabbit went to the library.
He chose a book about . . .

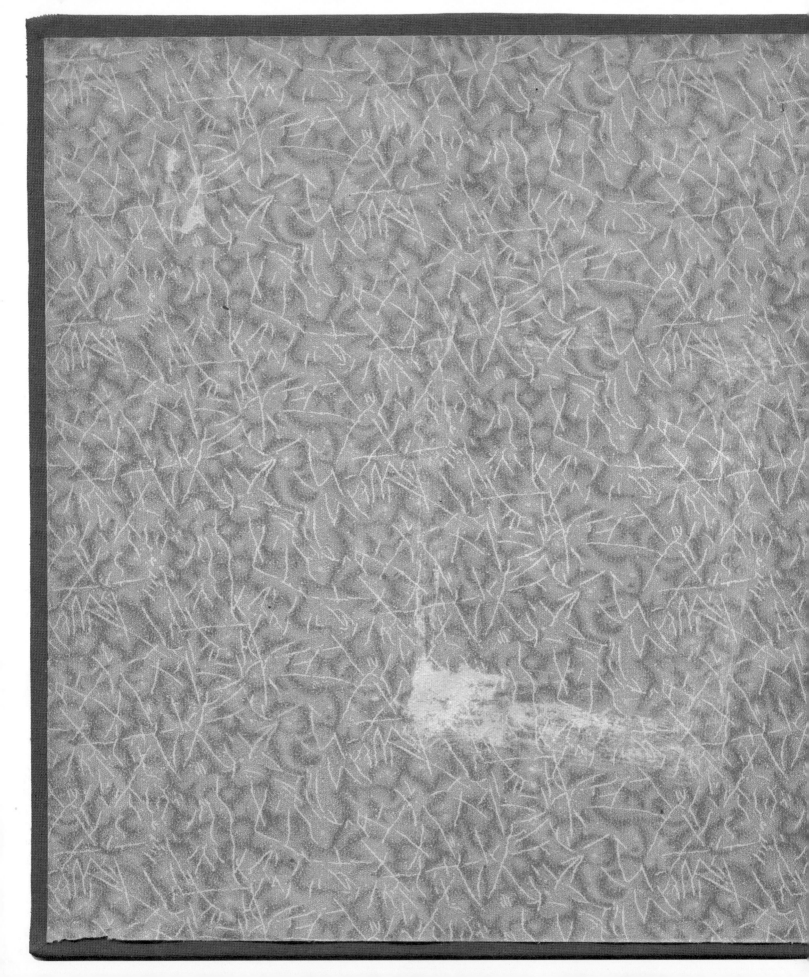

WEST BUCKS
PUBLIC BURROWING
LIBRARY
☎ 218-555-3210

Telephone 218-555-3210

West Bucks Public Burrowing Library

Please return or renew on or before the last date stamped
A fine may be charged if items are returned late

07/03/1991 →		
06/12/1992	04/26/1997	
10/02/1992		03/09/2002
12/07/1993	10/07/1997	
05/29/1994		05/08/2002
06/17/1995	02/14/1998	05/10/2003
		03/17/2004
08/20/1995	07/28/1998	
		04/04/2004
11/20/1996		02/12/2005
02/14/1997	09/22/2000	08/09/2005
		09/24/2005

GRAY WOLVES live in packs of between two and ten animals.

They can survive almost anywhere:
from the Arctic Circle . . .

. . . to the outskirts of towns and villages.

In some areas wolves have retreated
to places where fewer people live,
such as forests and woodland.

They have sharp claws...

. . . bushy tails . . .

. . . and dense fur, which harbors fleas and ticks.

An adult wolf has forty-two
teeth. Its jaws are twice as
powerful as those of a large dog.

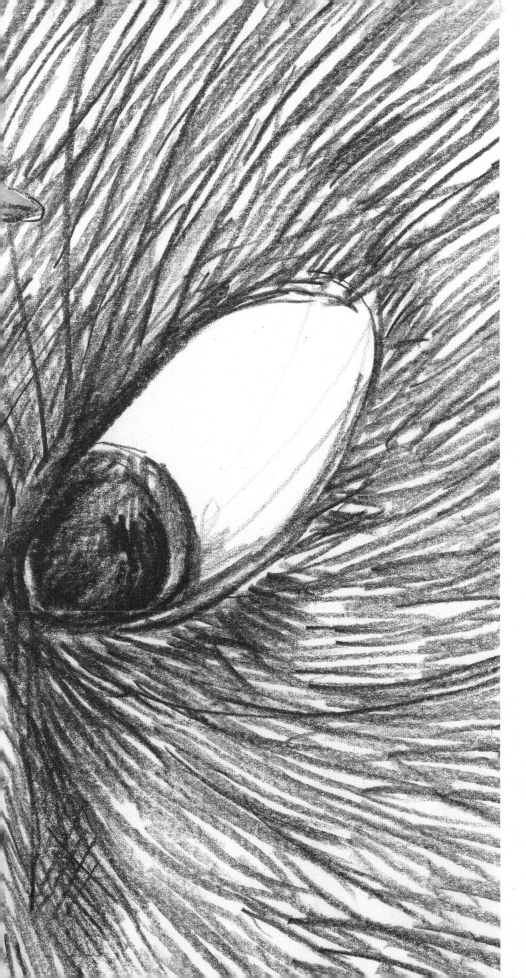

Wolves eat mainly meat. They hunt large prey such as deer, bison, and moose.

They also enjoy smaller mammals, like beavers, voles, and . . .

. . . rabbits.

The author would like to point out
that no rabbits were eaten during
the making of this book.
    It is a work of fiction.
    And so, for more sensitive readers,
here is an alternative ending.

Luckily this wolf was a vegetarian, so they
shared a jam sandwich, became the best of
friends, and lived happily ever after.

merciless
don collections

This matter is now URGENT & it is in your own
interest to contact us.
Please call us NOW at
800-555-0111

Registered Office
The Den
High Hill

PAYUP
No. 250000B

regards
R. Badger

Open Air 2004
Mai – September
Museumsplatz Bonn

G. RABBIT
LANE'S END BURROW
THE LONG FIELD
NIBBLESWICK
GREAT BURROW

BRIEFZENTRUM 53
15 –
Deutschland
55 €

JACK O'HARE
229 RABBIT RUN
THE BIG APPLE   01108
NIP CODE

Mr G. Rabbit
Lane's End Burrow
The Long Field
NIBBLESWICK
GREAT BURROW

VIA HARE MAIL
CORREO AEREO
PAR AVION

22 USA
22 USA

BUCKSPOOL

NEW ZEALAND
POSTAGE
999
PAID

RÉPUBLIQUE FRANÇAISE

NANTES
ROMAIN
26/09   17H   0003,00
44100   602 PC449...

The Long Field
Nibbleswick

M. G. Rabbit
Lane's End Burrow
The Long Field
Nibbleswick

BY AIR MAIL
PAR AVION
MIT LUFTPOST